Shadow of History

Steampunk OZ: Book 7

by Steve DeWinter

I0625872

Summary

In this action-packed second season of Steampunk OZ, American author S.D. Stuart returns to the Australis Penal Colony, where an ancient, and devastating, weapon was hidden a millennium ago.

Book 7

Caleb is ready to begin his perilous journey across OZ to restore Dorothy's memories. But the OZ he is returning to is not the same one he left.

This book is a work of fiction. References to real people, events, establishments, organization, or locales are intended only to provide a sense of authenticity, and are used fictitiously. All other characters, and all incidents and dialogue, are drawn from the author's imagination and are not to be construed as real.

eBook Edition

ISBN-10: 1-61978-044-5

ISBN-13: 978-1-61978-044-6

Paperback Edition

ISBN-10: 1-61978-045-3

ISBN-13: 978-1-61978-045-3

Chapter 1

The massive black locomotive sat on railroad tracks that started at the center of the large city and stretched all the way to the external defensive wall. It belched a cloud of steam that engulfed Caleb in a white shroud. He lost sight of Dorothy and the Tin Man for a brief moment until the hot vapor dissipated. When it cleared, he could see them standing with Toto on the other side of the town square from where he stood next to locomotive.

Ellis puffed furiously on his pipe, doing his best to compete with the locomotive, as he spoke to one of his men. "Have you been able to reach the Oracle?"

The tattoo covered soldier, not taking his eyes off the men unloading crates from the locomotive, shook his head. "No sir. The only thing we get on his frequency is static."

"Keep trying. I want to make sure our friends here are welcomed with open arms and not firearms."

"Yes sir."

The soldier ran off and Ellis placed a hand on the oversized wagon wheels that had been fitted to the locomotive. The wheels were as big around as he was tall. His fingers stroked the grooves carved at alternating angles along the edge of the ten-inch thick wheels.

"These grooves might give you a bit of a bumpy ride as you gain speed on the track, but that's nothing compared to the ride you'll get when you run out of track. These modified wheels should provide enough traction on the ground to keep you going through the siege camp, and all the way to the center of OZ before you run out of coal."

Caleb inspected the row of wheels mounted on the locomotive. He didn't know much about trains, but he knew they had to be on a track to get to where they were going. His eyes follow the tracks the locomotive rested on. They ended against the wall at the edge of the city. Men with shaved heads and tattoos worked tirelessly to clear away stones from the wall, leaving only one layer of protection between the city and the siege camp outside. This would give the locomotive minimal resistance when it hit the wall; and a big surprise for the bandits on the other side who had no idea what was coming.

Still, riding a wild out-of-control locomotive without a guide-track did not sound like the best idea Caleb had ever heard.

"How do we steer the train once we are off the tracks?"

Ellis chuckled. "You won't be needing to steer her. Think of this length of track as a gun barrel and the locomotive as a bullet. We've already aimed you in the right direction. You will just keep going in a straight line until she stops."

"What if we hit something?"

"You'll just go right on through it." He slapped a hand on Caleb's shoulder. "There ain't nothing in OZ that can stop this beast once she gets started. Trust me, you'll carve a path through everything in your way until you run out of steam. Now if you'll excuse me, I have a lot to do to get ready to deal with the big hole you're about to make in my wall."

Ellis walked off, smoke puffing up above his head as he moved away, like a smaller version of the locomotive.

As soon as Ellis disappeared into a building, Caleb was shoved hard from behind. He wasn't expecting it and stumbled forward into the side of the locomotive. He singed the fur on the palm of his hand as he braced himself against the boiler before regaining his balance and saving his hands from burning any longer than necessary. As if any amount of burning was necessary.

Tattoo Head, the same guy with the blackened teeth who had ordered them out of the carriage at gunpoint earlier, towered over him. He was easily a head taller than Caleb, and did not look happy.

"Who do you think you are?"

Caleb's inner fire had just been stoked and he curled his hands into fists ready for a fight. The spring-loaded sword shot out from the armor on his left arm. Tattoo took a step back as a dagger appeared in his own hand.

"You wanna dance? Let's dance."

Caleb relaxed his hands and the sword retracted back into the armor.

"I'm not your enemy."

"Are you sure of that! You've done more to hurt us in five hours than the enemy could in two months. Because of you, our defenses will be down for the first time, and my soldiers are already exhausted from dismantling the wall. We will be weak and vulnerable, and I don't think you're worth it."

"Ellis thinks I'm worth it."

"Ellis is a fool. He was not the only one who went up against the Directors and lost. Just because we were banished here does not mean we are out of the fight. We are the ones who've maintained our strength, discipline, and our sense of purpose. We should be going instead of you, a cowardly pussycat."

That was it.

The sword sprang back into action as he swung a tight arc through the air. Tattoo countered with his dagger.

The blades connected in midair with a clang.

They kicked up choking dust as they circled each other, their blades ringing as they slashed at each other, neither one of them hitting anything but the others' blade.

Tattoo was good. But there was a difference between a soldier trained for battle and an assassin trained to kill. While Tattoo was focused on besting him with the blade, Caleb was taking in the whole environment.

He heard the familiar ticking sound coming from the locomotive and knew what was coming next. He continued to slash at Tattoo with his sword, driving him backward toward the locomotive.

Right when the ticking sound stopped, Caleb swung his sword too wide, leaving an opening that Tattoo took with a knowing grin.

Caleb closed his eyes and dropped low just as the locomotive engulfed them both in steam.

As the steam cleared, everyone watching saw a surprised Tattoo flat on his back with Caleb resting the tip of his sword under his chin.

"The next time you call me a coward, you won't be able to finish the word."

A few halted claps morphed into a round of applause and cheers. Caleb wasn't the only one who hated Tattoo.

He tore his attention away from the soldier he had downed and watched the crowd split like the Red Sea before Moses as Ellis moved forward through the crowd. Ellis puffed on his pipe silently until Caleb retracted his sword and stood up.

Tattoo scrambled to his feet and stood at attention.

Ellis held the pipe to his lips, but did not puff on it as he regarded the soldier.

"How many men have you killed with your dagger in hand-to-hand combat?"

"Twenty-two, sir."

"Have you ever lost a fight?"

Tattoo flinched before responding. "No sir."

Ellis poked him in the chest with his pipe. "I hope this settles any debate as to why he was chosen."

"Yes sir."

"Good."

"And tell me, commander, what is the punishment for carrying a concealed blade inside my city walls?"

Tattoo stared straight ahead. "Death by hanging, sir."

"Is there a compelling reason I should not carry out that sentence immediately?"

Tattoo stood rigid. "The enemy is camped outside our front door. I have ordered the men to carry a weapon at all times. We must be prepared."

"Prepared for what?"

"The enemy getting in."

"Exactly. The enemy is outside those walls. He," Ellis pointed at Caleb, "is not the enemy. If anything, he is our one chance to stop an enemy even greater than those that surround our city. If it requires the destruction of this city, and the death of everyone here, so that this man and his friends can continue their journey, then that is what happens. Do I make myself clear?"

"Crystal, sir."

"Good."

A flash of light filled the sky followed by a massive boom that made everyone duck instinctively.

Ellis stared up at the dark clouds that stretched across the sky. "No, no, no, no, no. Not now."

Large drops of rain splattered against Caleb's face. He wiped them away quickly. The last thing he needed was rain to drench his fur. It took forever to dry out. Never mind the wonderful smell of wet fur. He had to get inside, and soon, to wait out the storm.

Ellis grabbed him and pushed him toward the locomotive while barking orders at his men. "Get the rest of his group. They are leaving now!"

Caleb understood why he disliked the rain, but what was Ellis's problem?

"Why the rush?"

Ellis didn't slow down as he guided Caleb quickly to the passenger compartment at the rear of the locomotive. "I lied earlier when I said nothing could stop this locomotive. If the rain keeps up, this whole area will be a slogging mud pit in no time. If the locomotive sinks into the mud, you're not going anywhere until the ground dries and we can dig it out. That could take months."

Ellis pushed Caleb up into the locomotive. Dorothy, the Tin Man, and Toto were being hurried across the town square by two of Ellis' tattooed soldiers.

The locomotive engineer snapped his fingers in front of Caleb's face to redirect his attention and pointed to various dials and readouts.

"That's the pressure gauge. That's the temperature gauge. Anytime the temperature drops below here," he pointed to a chalk mark drawn on the edge of the dial and then grabbed the handle of the firebox. "Lift and pull like this to open the firebox and shovel coal in. Be sure to lock it like this to keep the heat in the system.

"This is your throttle. The engine's primed and ready. As soon as everyone's inside, push it up gradually to gain speed. Once you get going, set it to full and forget about it.

"This is the brake. We're on level ground right now so it's not engaged. You're not going to need it this trip, so don't touch it. Momentum is your friend. Once you stop, it's really hard to get started back up again, so don't stop.

"When you run out of coal, and the pressure drops below this mark here," he pointed to another chalk line, "your ride is almost over. If you're lucky, she'll come to a nice, gradual stop."

He clapped the coal dust off his hands and looked around the engine room. "I guess that's it."

He slipped past Caleb and hopped out of the locomotive. Caleb called out after him. "Where are you going? I think we're just about to leave."

The engineer barked a laugh. "Oh, I'm not going with you."

"Who's going to drive the train?"

"It's not a train. It's a locomotive engine."

"What?"

"Never mind. I showed you everything you need to know. Good luck."

The engineer ran across the town square, tucking his head into the collar of his coat to protect it from the heavy rain while splashing through the widening puddles.

Ellis ushered the rest of Caleb's group up into the locomotive.

Caleb yelled down at him, "The engineer ran off!"

"All hell's going to break loose the second you go through that wall. I need every available man to deal with it."

Another one of the shaved and tattooed soldiers ran up to Ellis and shouted over the pounding rain. "The ground's softening too fast. In another minute, the tracks won't hold the engine's weight without buckling. If they don't leave now, they won't make it to the outer wall, let alone have enough speed to break through it."

Ellis nodded and gripped the door handle as he looked up at Caleb. "You heard the man. Time to get going." He slid the door closed, shutting the four of them inside; alone and on their own.

Again.

Someone banged on the outside of the door and a muffled voice said, "Go!"

Caleb gripped the throttle and pushed up. The locomotive vibrated from the grooves on the wheels as they spun in place. It finally surged forward as the wheels gained traction on the wet track.

They were moving!

He leaned out the engine window and could see the railroad tracks terminate at the wall half a kilometer away. Even with the wall reduced to only one stone thick, they would still feel it when they hit. They would need to find something to brace themselves with if they didn't want to be thrown around inside the engineer's compartment upon impact.

He pushed the throttle to half speed. At first, the wheels slipped with the increased surge from the pistons, but then they gripped the rails and propelled the locomotive faster down the track.

The locomotive vibrated like a carriage without spring-shocks on a cobblestone road. Caleb tightened his jaw to keep his teeth from clacking together too much.

As soon as he felt the locomotive settle into a steady rhythm, he shoved the throttle all the way past the full speed marking.

The pistons shrieked their displeasure with the sudden demand for more power, but they complied with their orders and pushed the locomotive beyond the advertised top speed.

As they rushed past, the blur of the larger commercial buildings in the inner part of the city gave way to the smaller blurs of the residential houses along the outskirts of town. At this speed, the locomotive never had a chance to settle into the grooves carved into the wheels, and it was a much smoother ride. The inertia of the locomotive building speed had lessened once they hit the fastest it could go, and it was easier to remain in place without using all his strength on the handhold.

The Tin Man had not been phased by any of this, and stood as if he were in the middle of a wide open field on a calm sunny afternoon.

Dorothy crouched in the corner of the engineer's compartment with one arm wrapped around a handhold and her other arm wrapped around Toto.

Caleb tried to smile reassuringly as he hollered over the rat-a-tat of the wheels on the track. "Are you okay?"

Her voice's staccato rhythm matched the vibrations of the locomotive. "Is it going to be like this the whole way?"

Caleb hadn't thought of that before, but she was probably right. This gave all the indications of an ill-thought plan. And they hadn't hit the worst of it yet.

Speaking of the worst part of this plan, he leaned back out the window. They were a quarter kilometer from the wall; and still gaining speed.

Something closer along the track caught his eye.

Not along the track.

On the track!

A horse drawn cart had become trapped in the mud, half of it still blocking the track and overladen with straw. The cart's owner was furiously working to unhitch his horse from the cart. He already knew what Caleb had just discovered. The cart was bogged down in the mud and wasn't going anywhere until the locomotive hit it. The owner didn't want to lose his horse at the same time.

Caleb's hand was on the brake when the engineer's words came back to him. Momentum was his friend. They needed to maintain speed to blast through the wall and beyond. If this locomotive was to act like a bullet shot from a gun, he couldn't stop it midway. Even if he pulled the brake immediately, he would still hit the cart at three-quarters of the engine's top speed.

He let go of the brake and, numb from the constant vibration of the wheels, never felt the impact. He only saw the cloud of straw and wood fragments shoot past the window.

He looked back and a wave of relief washed over him. The owner struggled to hold the reins of his terrified, but still alive, horse while he considered the splintered remains of his livelihood.

Up ahead, the track was empty.

It was clear sailing all the way to the solid granite castle wall.

Chapter 2

Outside the city, in the siege camp, two bandits huddled under an already soaked canvas in the pouring rain.

"This buggers all," the first one said.

"You're telling me. We've been out here for months and nothin'," replied the second.

"Yeah, we were promised money and women."

The second bandit mocked looking around him. "I don't see any money."

The first bandit laughed. "Or women."

The second bandit shivered and tugged his waterlogged coat tighter. "I'm sick of this waiting around. I wish something, anything, would happen."

It was at that moment the castle wall exploded.

Inside the locomotive, everyone was thrown forward from the impact, but they still managed to cling to their handholds. The prep work by Ellis' tattooed soldiers had proven to be well-thought-out indeed. The castle wall offered little resistance to the speeding locomotive. In fact, for the passengers inside, it was a minor bump in an already rough ride.

The locomotive barreled through the siege camp, tossing bandits left and right, and tore through the shoddy structures as if they weren't even there. The grooves of the oversized wheels dug into the mud, the locomotive propelling itself out the other side of the siege camp.

Within minutes, the locomotive crested the low hill and picked up speed as it headed down the other side. Once out of sight, the castle and the surrounding siege camp were but a distant memory.

There were more immediate needs that took Caleb's full attention away from worrying about what they left behind. The needle on the temperature gauge slowly crawled to the chalk line. If it passed the line, they would begin to slow down; and momentum could be their enemy just as well as their friend.

"We need to add more coal to the fire," he yelled out to the engine room in general. Dorothy's face was buried in Toto's fur. Toto slit his eyes and bared his teeth with a curl of a lip. Neither of them were going to help.

The Tin Man held up the three-fingered claw that served as his hand. "I'm not built for holding a shovel."

The needle swept past the chalk mark and Caleb wasn't sure if he could really sense it, or if he only imagined that the locomotive was slowing down. It didn't matter if he imagined it or not. If the temperature kept dropping in the firebox, the steam pressure would drop, and they would eventually stop. If they were going to continue on their journey, it was up to him to do something about it.

He unhooked the shovel from its tether, the only thing keeping it from flying out the window on their wild ride. He would have to remember to reconnect it or else they would lose the shovel entirely.

He shoveled coal into the firebox and slammed the lid closed.

The scenery rushed by the window. They had been bumping along through it for so long, he became used to the floor of the engineer's compartment trying to knock him to the ground, and it no longer felt like a wild ride through the countryside.

Everyone, not just him, had quickly adapted to their new environment.

The Tin Man seemed at ease, standing in the corner. It would probably take a lot more than careening through OZ in an out-of-control locomotive to make him come unhinged.

Toto was providing comfort for Dorothy, but he probably hadn't been programmed to experience fear, so the situation they currently found themselves in was of little consequence.

Dorothy, also, was becoming more comfortable with their bouncing ride and no longer huddled with her face buried in Toto's fur. She even caught Caleb looking at her a few times, but he always felt embarrassed for staring so long, smiled, and looked back out the window.

Despite looking away each time, he still watched her out of the corner of his eye.

The Tin Man and Toto, he had just met. And thanks to the actions of the Southern Marshal, Dorothy was also a stranger. Despite knowing what the Southern Marshal had done to her, it still felt strange that he knew her so well and yet she did not recognize him.

Every time he looked at her, the flood of memories of what they shared together ran through his mind. But because she had been turned into a scarecrow, he didn't see the same emotions from her when they made eye contact.

If they didn't succeed in getting the weapon, and returning it to the Southern Marshal, Dorothy might stay this way; forever.

He jumped when someone tapped him on the shoulder. His eyes focused on Dorothy, who had knelt in front of him.

"I'm sorry, I didn't mean to startle you."

He snapped the shovel's tether onto the hook and futilely tried to wipe the coal dust from his hands. "It's okay. I was lost in thought and didn't notice you."

"Well I've noticed you watching me."

Caleb's heart felt like it was being squeezed. "I'm sorry about that."

She gripped his hands in hers. "No. Don't be. I was told, when I first woke up, that my memory had been erased and I would get it back when we finished this task. I take it, from how you keep looking at me and turning away, we knew each other before."

"We did."

"How well did we know each other?"

Now his heart was being twisted around unnaturally inside his rib cage. He didn't know how much to tell her. Or how much he should tell her.

"Caleb?"

She snapped him out of his reverie again. She looked up at him with innocent eyes.

"How well did we know each other?"

"We were very good friends."

"This must be hard for you. I don't remember you at all. I actually don't remember much of anything."

He gripped her hands tightly and gave her a reassuring smile.

"Don't worry. We will get your memory back; no matter what."

She returned his smile. "I won't have to live out my days as a scarecrow?"

"Not if I can help it."

Dorothy clung to the hand rail and stared out at the passing scenery as the locomotive rocketed through OZ. She searched the horizon for something that would jog her memory, any memory, of the life she had lived before waking up this morning.

For several hours, the scenery gradually shifted from one type of terrain to another. A few times, they passed close enough to a town to make out the individual stones of the varied buildings and houses but, fortunately for the inhabitants of these cities, their uncontrolled journey did not take them directly through the center of town for any of them.

Caleb slammed the firebox door shut. "Well, that's the last of our coal. All we can do now is wait for this ride to end."

They smiled briefly at each other before they each returned to looking out their respective windows. Dorothy tried to conjure up any feelings she had for Caleb, but came up empty. She tried desperately to remember something, anything, from before today. But each time she thought she might have caught a glimpse of some old memory, it faded into oblivion before she could focus on it.

She had been put into an impossible situation. She woke up with no memory of who she was or how she got there, with people she never remembered meeting before, telling her who to trust and what to do to get her memory restored.

She didn't have any reasons to trust anyone. She also didn't have any reasons to distrust anyone, other than her lack of memories. But was that reason enough to distrust everyone? With the exception of Toto, who had followed her everywhere ever since she awoke, the three of them were on this quest under one form of duress or another.

They were all in this together. But, they each had different reasons to be here. And while she couldn't fully understand why this frightened her, it did.

However, nothing frightened her more than the Tin Man. Whenever she looked in his direction, she always found herself staring at the sharp, claw-like hands. Claws that could cut her in half with a single swiping motion. She shook her head and tried not to dwell on such things. Fortunately, the Tin Man had moved to the roof of the locomotive a couple of hours earlier. He said he wanted to watch the path ahead, to keep an eye out for any signs of trouble. She didn't care why he went up to the roof. As long as it kept him, and his claws, as far away from her as possible.

Whatever programming was used for the Tin Man, she hoped it was not prone to insanity. Why was she thinking like that? She had to be positive if they were going to succeed in their quest.

Just as she was trying to banish the negative thoughts from her mind, the Tin Man jumped down into the engineer's compartment, grabbed Caleb in a huge claw and threw him off the locomotive.

Dorothy's scream caught in her throat as the Tin Man reached for her and Toto.

Chapter 3

Before his mind could even properly register the fact that the Tin Man had thrown him out of the locomotive, Caleb hit the ground at high speed. His armored suit hardened instantly and he tumbled several hundred feet across the sun-baked ground before coming to a stop on his back.

Something streaked across the sky in his field of vision, leaving behind a trail of fire and black smoke. A shrieking sound pierced his eardrums and hackled the fur over his entire body.

The head splitting scream was coming from the fireball, and judging by the angle of smoke trailing behind it in the wide arc it made across the sky, it was coming back down to the ground.

He sat up and focused his attention on the screaming fireball.

His mouth went dry when it impacted with the locomotive and exploded.

The shock wave shoved him back several feet, his armor easily deflecting the shards of thick cast iron that tried to impale him with their twisted shards.

He regained his footing and gawked at the meters wide crater where he last saw the locomotive. For the next minute, twisted pieces of metal, each no bigger than his fist, dropped out of the sky. Whatever hit the locomotive, had exploded with more destructive force than he had ever seen before in his life.

However, the shrieking sound was something he had heard before.

And it never meant anything good.

He heard the whooshing sound of jump jets right before the Tin Man, holding a terrified Dorothy and struggling Toto in each bent arm, landed near him. He didn't bother releasing them and instead surveyed the crater where the locomotive used to be. "What the hell was that?"

Caleb scanned the skies for more trouble. "I don't know, but I have an idea of who sent it. I hope, for all our sakes, I'm wrong."

He saw them moments before their wailing sounds reached him.

He was not wrong.

They flew through the sky, born on black and brown stained canvas wings, like large bats against the pale blue sky. Even at this distance he recognized the cone shaped face masks that came to a sharp point, like the beak of a bird, and the large plume of black feathers extending out from their helmets.

But the dead giveaway, of who was fast approaching, were the black steel gauntlets worn over their left hands. The elongated metal claws always sharpened to a razor's edge and dipped in poison before they engaged the enemy.

Their name alone was enough to send even the hardest criminals in OZ into a flurry of blind panic. It was a word rarely spoken in hushed whispers or during polite conversation.

It was usually screamed in terror.

Caleb screamed that word right now. "Banshees!"

The five Banshees adjusted their angle of flight when they spotted the survivors from the obliterated locomotive.

A quick glance around proved Caleb's worst fear. There was nowhere to run, and there was nowhere to hide.

His sword and gun sprang out at his nonverbal commands while the Tin Man set Dorothy and Toto down.

Without a single word passing between them, Caleb, Toto and the Tin Man placed themselves between Dorothy and the coming threat.

And prepared for the worst.

Because the worst was coming.

The Banshees landed ten meters away, shed their canvas wings, and extended their clawed hands. They did not rely on brute force to overcome their enemies. They relied on their speed and agility. And they let the poison dripping from the tips of their extended claws do most of the heavy lifting. One scratch was an assured, and painful, death sentence. Caleb's special armor might protect him from the claws, but he still had exposed skin at every joint that still left him vulnerable. The only ones immune to any kind of poison were Toto and the Tin Man. With the two automatons, and his armored suit, they might stand a chance against the five Banshees.

Worse than the screeching that signaled their impending arrival was their silence as they moved in for the kill.

Toto was the first react. He charged at the closest Banshee, growling and snarling fiercely. He leaped through the air and the Banshee caught him with her clawed hand. He let out a terrified yelp and dropped to the ground, lifeless.

The Tin Man raised his gun and fired. The Banshees scattered in every direction, each one avoiding the steady barrage of bullets. One held up her clawed hand and sparks of lightning shot out to engulf the Tin Man. He stopped firing, and fell face down into the dirt.

These Banshees had upgraded their gauntlets to deal with automatons. With both his strongest members down and out for the count, and with all five Banshees still untouched, he was not going to win this fight. The only way to protect Dorothy, and save himself, was to get as far away from them as possible.

He spun around and bear-hugged Dorothy. He crouched and felt the jump jets engage right before every muscle in his body constricted.

Still gripping Dorothy, they both collapsed into the dust.

He and Dorothy stared at each other, unable to move. He was not unconscious, but had no control over anything. He couldn't turn his head. He couldn't move his eyes. He couldn't even blink.

It took three Banshees working together to pry them apart and lay them each on their backs.

A Banshee entered his field of vision and removed her metal beak. If he still had voluntary control over his body, he would've gasped in surprise. He knew that only women were allowed in the ranks of the Banshees, but he hadn't expected any of them to be so beautiful.

They were ruthless killers, and it was rare that anyone saw them without their mask. He had expected them to look more mannish.

Maybe he'd listened too long to the drunken rationalizations of men in pubs, discussing why a woman would choose to become a Banshee. They always seemed to settle on the same reason. She must be as ugly as a mule and couldn't find herself a man.

Clearly, as he stared up at the smooth features of her face, that was not the case. She spoke softly to him, like a mother tending to a sleepy child.

"I'm going to close your eyes now. We wouldn't want them to dry out."

She swiped her hand across his face and the world became nothing more than a bright orangish hue as sunlight filtered through his eyelids.

As he lie perfectly still on the ground, he listened to the Banshees speak to each other in a language he'd never heard before. It was a lilting, breathy language that seemed to be very old, and not as consonant heavy as the modern languages.

He heard wagon wheels crunching on the hard ground and sensed, rather than felt since he still had no control or feeling of his body, the motion of being lifted and placed in the wagon. It must've been a covered wagon, because the light filtering in through his eyelids darkened slightly.

It was unsettling to be awake and aware, yet not be able to move or feel any part of your body. The only senses he had were sight and sound. He could not feel anything, but he could hear his heartbeat, and his breathing and swallowing at regular intervals. Even though he lost control of his body, at least the involuntary functions were still working.

The sense he missed the most, was smell. He hadn't realized how much he relied on it to gauge his surroundings until it was gone.

He always closed his eyes upon entering a new city so that he could memorize the smells. Every city had its unique smell and he was able, during the few times he'd been hooded and whisked away to meet a contact in a secret location, to know exactly where he was.

For the first time in his life, he was flying blind and had no idea where they were taking him.

Or why.

He tried to focus on possible reasons why they destroyed the locomotive and captured them. But not being able to feel one's own body was too distracting. His mind wandered too easily from the lack of stimulus. Reduced to the single reddish color of his eyelids and the random sounds around him, his brain struggled to reconstruct the rest of his environment. But rather than try to reconstruct the environment around him, he instead hallucinated that he was seated at the dinner table back in Nero's casino, years ago.

He could smell the food. He could turn his head and look all around the dining hall like he was there.

But none of it was real, and he forced himself to focus on the sounds around him rather than let his brain create a new reality.

The rumbling of the wooden wagon wheels shifted tempo as they moved from a dirt road to cobblestone pavement.

He had no way of judging which city they had just entered, because he had no way of knowing how long they had been traveling, or at what speed.

The only indication that time had passed was the gradual darkening on the other side of his eyelids. He couldn't hear Dorothy in the wagon next to him, or anyone from the rest of his group. Which made sense. He couldn't speak himself, so none of them would be making any noise.

A chilling thought suddenly occurred to him. What if they had been split up? What if Dorothy, the Tin Man, Toto, and he were sent to different locations?

His mind grabbed that thought and propelled him beyond the boundaries of sanity. He used all his will to force himself back to reality. He focused on the details of his quest, which only made him angry about his current situation.

His imagination took over and showed him a world where a select group of humans used the ancient hybrid's weapon to subjugate everyone on the planet. It was worse than he could've ever imagined. It wasn't a world united. It wasn't heaven. It was hell.

He forced himself back to reality again. He had to do something.

How long was his body going to be frozen like this?

If they would only let him speak, he could tell them how important it was to them, and to all of OZ, that his group be allowed to keep going without interference. Precious time had been wasted already, and he was frantic to get to the Brahmastra before the humans did, now more than ever.

The wheels stopped grinding over cobblestones and fell silent. Several voices exchanged comments in that strange language before someone said something he understood.

The voice was very close, as if its speaker was inspecting him from only a few inches away.

"You're right. Maybe this is the half-human half-animal creature the Oracle spoke of. Wake him up."

Every muscle in his body constricted and knotted up. The tingling sensation started in his fingers and toes, and worked its way up through his arms and legs. His equilibrium was shot to hell and his head spun wildly. When his face felt numb, he thought about opening his eyes and he did.

He was seated, tied to a chair. His brain registered he was no longer lying down and his equilibrium reset. Once properly oriented, the room stopped spinning.

He tested moving his head by looking around the room. Slowly at first to fend off the waves of nausea that washed over him with each motion. His neck was stiff, but at least he could still move it with some effort.

Off to his right, a couple of women inspected pieces of armor that looked exactly like his.

He tilted his head down to look at his chest and legs.

It was his armor.

Fortunately, he was still dressed in the brown leather under-suit. He hadn't been stripped naked. Of course, with fur covering his entire body, he really couldn't be naked. Technically speaking.

Three more women were in an animated discussion on the far side of the room. And by animated, it looked like they were arguing over something. Most likely, they were arguing over him.

With feeling returning to normal, he tested the bindings that held him to the chair. While the ropes were not tight enough to restrict blood flow, they had very little play. He would not be wriggling out of them anytime soon.

One of the three women noticed him tugging on his ropes and walked over. The two with her, followed close behind.

She stood with her hands on her hips, a fire burning in her eyes. "I'd like you to give Ellis a message for me."

He wasn't sure what he had expected her to say to him, but this caught him totally off guard.

"Huh?"

She punched him across the face, his teeth rattling from the impact. He flexed his jaw as the heat level rose on the left side of his face.

"You tell him, the next time he sends a bomb headed directly toward my city, he will not live to see another sunrise."

"What are you…"

She struck him again. This time, he felt his brain bounce around inside his skull. She didn't look very muscular, but she hit like someone twice her size. Her hand flashed back across his vision and he noticed the glint of metal from something gripped in her hand.

She bent down to speak to him at eye level.

"I will give you the night to regain your strength and recover from your," she gripped his chin in her hand and inspected her handiwork. "Accidental fall down the stairs."

One of the two women who'd been inspecting his armor approached. He recognized her is the same one who closed his eyes immediately after they attacked. She had those same bright blue eyes with pinpoint dark pupils that were unforgettable. "Ma'am, do you think the Oracle will want to speak with him?"

The one who punched him across the face looked ready to hit Blue Eyes. "The Oracle is an idiot. We are no longer going to do what he says. I'm in charge now, and if anyone has a problem with that, my door is always open to hear complaints."

She looked around, challenging anyone to question her self-appointed leadership. The other woman lowered their heads.

Caleb had just witnessed a shift in power. It didn't sound like a change for the better.

She regarded him with an evil grin.

"Very well. Put him in the dungeon with the others. Tomorrow morning, we will send back just enough of him to deliver our message."

Chapter 4

Deep in the bowels of Center City, Caleb was pushed into a jail cell. He stumbled, but quickly regained his balance.

The bars clanked shut behind him.

The two Banshee guards whispered to each other in their strange language and laughed at their private joke as they headed back up the stairs.

Dorothy sat on the dirt floor of the same jail cell with her back against the wall. Toto's head was in her lap and she stroked the fur along the back of his neck. He didn't react to her attention, or to Caleb entering the cell.

The electrical shock from the Banshee gauntlet must have fried his electrical circuits. Whether it was permanent, there was no way to tell. Caleb wondered if the Tin Man had fared any better.

Caleb crouched down next to her. "Are you okay?"

"I'm doing better than Toto. Where are we?"

"You don't remember this place?"

She looked around her at the bare stone walls. "Should I?"

"We've been here before. We're in the dungeon of the Wizard's Castle. We've only been gone for six months, but it doesn't seem like Scarecrow is in charge any longer.

Ellis mentioned that everything has gotten worse around OZ, in just the past couple of months. I wonder what's been happening out here since we left?"

A new voice outside the cell answered his question. "The Oracle can answer that."

He stared through the bars of the cell into same bright blue eyes of the one who had risked standing up against the self-appointed Banshee leader. She had backed down quickly, but here she was again. And most likely breaking some rule coming to see them.

"You're the one who kept my eyes from drying out."

She grinned at being recognized. "My name's Tara."

"You mentioned this Oracle before. Who is he?"

"He is the Oracle. He looks like an ordinary man, but he fell from the sky as a gift to us from the gods. The only reason the High Priestess did not order his immediate death is that he came to us broken. It was my task to nurse him back to health so he could stand trial for his crimes."

"What crimes?"

"It didn't matter. He was a man in OZ, and therefore, must have committed crimes against someone, somewhere."

This was the most absurd thing he'd ever heard in his life. And he grew up in OZ, so nothing should have surprised him. "You were going to put him on trial under the assumption he had committed a crime?"

"Children were not born in OZ until after the first few years. Reason dictates, everyone over the age of twenty was sent to OZ for committing a crime. So, logically, he had crimes he needed to be punished for. But I was able to convince the High Priestess that he was not an ordinary man. That he was a gift from the gods."

"A gift from the gods?"

"I told you. He fell from the sky."

"So, after you nursed him back to health he was put on trial?"

"No. He talked in his sleep through many a fevered dream and spoke of a life outside of OZ. A life that did not involve crime. And he knew things that only the creator of OZ could know. He spoke of the creator as if he knew him personally. I convinced the High Priestess that he was not here because of judgment, so we could not judge him further."

"How did he become the Oracle?"

"He gave the High Priestess information in exchange for his life. She sent us out on raiding parties to obtain the special equipment he requested. Equipment he used to show us what was happening all over OZ, in real time. It was the Oracle who showed us your locomotive being filled with explosives last week before departing the city in the south."

Explosives? Those must've been the crates he saw men unloading from the locomotive. Of course. There was no way he could have laid down the track and positioned the locomotive in such a short time. Ellis had told him to think of the track as a gun with the locomotive as a bullet. The reason he used that example was because it was a bullet. An explosive bullet they had planned to use.

But use against who?

With the exception of the siege camp, the first thing they'd come across since leaving the city was here.

At the Southern Marshal's insistence, Ellis had re-purposed his weapon originally designed for an attack on Center City.

He shook his head. "They removed the explosives to make room for us. It was no longer a weapon."

"They didn't remove enough. The bomb we hit the locomotive with could never have made an explosion that big. The best we could hope for was to knock it off course, away from the city. I could tell, from how you looked at what was left of your locomotive, you had no idea of its original purpose."

She inserted a key into the lock and swung open the cell bars.

He searched her hands for a weapon that she might be hiding in the jumble of clothes held in her arms. "What are you doing?"

"I'm taking you to see the Oracle."

She tossed the bundle of clothes at him. "Your friend needs to put these on."

He inspected the clothes. It was a Banshee outfit. "Why does she have to wear this?"

"If we want to make it through the city without being stopped, she has to look like one of us; and you have to be her prisoner."

"Prisoner?"

She held up a pair of rusted shackles. "The only men within the city walls are either prisoners, or slaves. Nothing will arouse suspicion faster than you freely walking around."

Dorothy looked down at Toto lying on the ground.

"What about him?"

Tara shook her head.

"I'm sorry. It will arouse too much suspicion if we carry the robot dog around the city. We have to leave him behind."

As they stepped out into the street, Dorothy tugged on the chain and the shackles bit into his wrists. He grunted in pain.

She flinched and dropped her end of the chain. "Sorry."

Tara swiftly picked up the chain and placed it back into Dorothy's hands. "No, that was good. The more he is mistreated, the less we will be noticed."

Caleb looked around at the people walking through the streets of the city. He saw mostly women. A few men, probably servants of the extravagantly dressed women they hurried along behind, followed with their heads bowed and eyes cast to the ground.

He had expected to see everyone dressed as Banshees. But the only two dressed like that were Dorothy and Tara.

He immediately worried they would stand out before realizing that when someone noticed them, they immediately turned their head away. Apparently, Banshees were just as feared by the people they protected as they were by the people they attacked.

Tara moved forward, the other pedestrians making a column of empty sidewalk for her almost instinctively, since none of them pretended to notice her.

They followed her through the city while Dorothy tugged on the chain a little more forcefully. "Keep moving, prisoner."

Caleb said through gritted teeth, "You're enjoying this a little too much."

He couldn't tell whether or not she smiled behind her beak shaped mask, but her eyes housed the tiny sparkle of the Dorothy he once knew. They made their way quickly through the city, ignored by everyone they came across. Tara, always a few steps ahead, scouted around each corner before motioning for Dorothy and Caleb to follow.

Tara slowed down. "Just a few more blocks. We're almost there."

She looked both ways across a busy street and then motioned for them to follow. They were halfway across another of the multitude of intersections they had crossed in the expansive city when Tara rushed back, shoved them into a back alley, and ushered them behind piles of rotting vegetables. The stench of decay and decomposition assaulted his nose. Right about now, it would be nice if his body was still numb so he could not smell the rot around him.

Tara was oblivious to, or just plain ignored, the smell as she peered around the corner. He sidled up next to her and peeked around the corner.

Down the street, in the direction she was looking, he saw two Banshees standing guard at the threshold of a dilapidated wooden door that looked to be the street-side entrance to the moss-covered stone house.

Caleb let out an exasperated breath. "Let me guess. That's the Oracle's house."

He and Tara exchanged a look and his shoulders drooped with the realization he was right.

She studied the two guards blocking their goal. "I didn't think you'd be noticed missing from the dungeon so quickly."

"What makes you think they know we're missing already?"

"The High Priestess only orders guards for the Oracle when there's trouble. I had to take us around the city in a non-direct route, or else we would have been discovered by now. Unfortunately, it also gave her time to put them in place."

She stared for a few more seconds before she turned around and clapped her hands on her thighs. "Doesn't matter. We have to get in there."

She seemed to notice the smell for the first time as a sly smile spread across her lips. She bent down, scooping up handfuls of rotting garbage before she stood up again. She held her hands stretched out on either side like a scale, as if comparing the weight of the garbage in her two hands.

He did not like the look in her eyes as she took a step toward him.

He took a step back and pulled the chain tight, Dorothy still holding the other end.

"What are you planning to do with that garbage?"

Tara never took her eyes off his. "If we expect those guards to believe we brought you to clean the Oracle's sewer, you have to smell the part."

She smeared the garbage into his clothes and fur. Dorothy refused to do anything except hang on to her end of the chain. He didn't want to pull her off balance, so he could do nothing more than stand there and let Tara smear him with garbage.

When she was done, she took a step back and admired her handiwork.

Caleb took short, halting breaths. His nose had not yet begun the process of ignoring the, now permanent, smell. "Was this absolutely necessary?"

"Yes. But you might have trouble making new friends for a while."

Feeling confident in her new plan, she led them straight to the Oracle's front door and stopped right in front of the other two Banshees. "Hey Leslie. Hey Melissa. Have you two met Cynthia yet? She's my new apprentice."

One of the guards stepped forward and blocked her with a hand. "What are you doing here, Tara?"

"It's the monthly cleaning."

Leslie pointed a finger at Caleb. "Who's that?"

Caleb followed the behavior he'd seen from the other men in the city and kept his stare fixated on his feet. The hooded cloak Tara had given him covered the feline features of his face as long as his head remained lowered.

Tara turned and regarded Caleb as if it was the first time she had taken notice of him. "The regular cleaner is sick, so I grabbed a sewer rat for the job. If you'll please let me by…"

Leslie stepped sideways and re-blocked Tara from entering the Oracle's house. "I don't know if you've heard, but the prisoners have escaped. The High Priestess thinks they might try to harm the Oracle."

Tara let a surprised expression wash over her face as she looked up and down the street. "Is it just the two of you?"

Leslie shrugged her shoulders. "Banshees are stationed at key points all around the city. They'll be caught long before they make it here."

Tara suddenly sounded agitated. "I was one of the five that captured them. They directly threatened the Oracle before we shocked them. You need to go immediately and bring more Banshees here."

Leslie stood her ground. "The High Priestess personally ordered us to stand guard at the Oracle's door. Why don't you go?"

Tara leaned in, their faces coming within inches of each other. "Are you refusing the direct order of a superior?"

Leslie stammered her reply. "No ma'am."

"Good. We will stand here with Melissa. Let's pray, for your sake, the enemy doesn't get here before you return with reinforcements."

Leslie snapped to attention. "Yes ma'am!"

She ran off without looking back.

Tara watched her disappear around the corner before facing Melissa. "I'm sorry about this."

Before Melissa could ask what Tara was sorry for, she grabbed Melissa with her left hand and hit her with an electrical charge from the gauntlet. Melissa was unconscious before she hit the ground.

Tara pushed open the front door to the Oracle's house and dragged the unconscious Banshee inside. Caleb and Dorothy rushed in after her. Tara looked up and down the street to verify nobody had seen what happened before closing the door.

She unlocked the manacles from Caleb's wrists.

"You don't have much time. Leslie is a good soldier and I just lit a fire under her. We've got, maybe, two minutes before she's back with more Banshees. You don't want to be here when that happens."

He glanced around the room. The house was nothing more than a single great room sparsely populated with furniture, only one door, the one they had come in through, and nobody else in the room but them. It looked lived in, but something looked off about the room. He couldn't place his finger on it, though. Something was wrong with the room, but he couldn't figure out what.

A fire burned in the fireplace and steam rose from a bowl of half eaten soup on the table. It looked like somebody had just left. But they had come in the only door, and certainly hadn't passed anyone going out on their way in. Somebody had recently placed that soup there. And then miraculously disappeared. Whoever was about to sit down for lunch had been interrupted by their entry, but had inexplicably disappeared.

That's what was missing from the room!

He looked around at the few pieces of furniture. They were all tables and shelves. There were no chairs anywhere. Why were there no chairs?

Tara propped the unconscious Melissa against a wall and hurried over to the fireplace. She waved frantically into the gaping maw of the fireplace. "Go through, the Oracle's waiting for you on the other side."

Caleb felt the heat from the fire all the way across the room. Even if he tried to run through it, his fur would ignite in an instant. Maybe their escape had been a ruse this whole time. He knew nothing about the woman who had helped them. This could all be part of some elaborate plan to kill them as escaped prisoners on the run.

They were being given a choice. Stay here and be captured, and most likely killed, or burn to death in the oversized fireplace. Either choice had the same outcome. Death.

Dorothy had been following obediently without complaint since they left the dungeon. She stopped in the middle of the room and pointed at the roaring fire.

"You want us to go in there?"

Tara glanced into the fireplace. "Oops."

She grabbed a crudely shaped candlestick off the mantel and pushed it into a gap between the stones at the base of the mantel shelf. It fit the gap perfectly. The flames receded and went out. The scraping of stone on stone revealed a door opening in the back of the fireplace.

Tara turned to them with a smile. "Sorry about that. Is this better?"

He grabbed Dorothy to keep her from running into the fireplace. He scanned the eyes of the Banshee, looking for a reason why she would betray her own people. "Why are you helping us?"

"The Oracle told me the truth about OZ."

"What truth?"

There was a bang on the front door followed by shouting and more banging. The door was old. It wouldn't stand up much longer to the abuse from outside. Tara tore her gaze from the splintering door and pleaded with him. "The Oracle will explain everything. You have to go now."

He and Dorothy rushed through the fireplace and into the darkened passageway that led down and away from the house. He took two steps before he realized it was still only he and Dorothy in the passageway. He turned back and poked his head through the opening.

"Aren't you coming with us?"

"No. I have to slow them down so you can escape."

"What are you going to do?"

She yanked the candlestick from the hole and the stone door started to slide closed. "Whatever it takes."

As if by magic, the flames reignited moments before the secret passageway sealed itself off from the rest of the house. With a loud clank, they were plunged into darkness.

His eyes adjusted as best they could, but there was no light in the passageway. He bumped his head several times before remembering that the passage had a low ceiling. He crouched as he made his way carefully down the gently sloping tunnel. In the pitch black tunnel, he didn't want to step off into empty air and find himself tumbling down a flight of stairs, so he tested the ground in front of him lightly as they moved forward slowly.

Dorothy's whisper broke the silence. "Caleb?"

"Yes. I'm here."

"You knew me before my memory was wiped, right?"

"Yes."

"Was I as afraid of the dark then as I am now?"

He groped back into the blackness. "Here. Hold my hand."

He heard the faint rustle of her Banshee suit before her hand brushed his, and she clamped on tight.

In the dark it was hard to tell, but he had been counting each step silently as they made their way through the tunnel. He guessed they had traveled just under a hundred feet without a single turn or any stairs. Just how long was this tunnel?

His foot probed forward and bumped into something. Had he finally reached some stairs heading upward?

He felt forward with this hand and came up against a wall.

He felt around him on both sides and in front. There were no passageways leading off in another direction. The only direction without a wall was the way they had just come.

They were at a dead end with nowhere to go. They certainly couldn't go back to where the Banshees would be waiting for them. At least not right away.

They could sit and wait for a while before making their way back up the tunnel. If they waited long enough, maybe the Banshees would leave the empty house and they could get away.

Dorothy was dressed like a Banshee. She could easily sneak past them on her own. And then what?

That wouldn't work. They had to stay together. But they couldn't stay here at the end of this tunnel forever. The Directors were still coming and he had to get the weapon before they did. He didn't have time to wait around in the dark for something to happen.

He had to make something happen. And he had to make it happen soon.

Who would build a secret passageway that didn't go anywhere? There must be something that opened a door at this end. He just had to find it.

He let go of Dorothy's hand and she let out a small yelp.

"I'm right here, Dorothy. Help me feel around the walls for something that might open the door. A lever or a push plate or something."

Together they felt and pushed on the stones that made up the walls, bumping into each other on occasion.

Dorothy's voice echoed softly in the low tunnel. "I think I found something."

A clunk sounded in the distance and the sound of rocks grinding against each other was followed by a faint light illuminating the tunnel from the newly created opening.

"Good work Dorothy."

He grabbed her hand and they slipped through the widening door before the grinding sound even stopped. Who knows how long it would remain open, and he didn't want it to start closing on them before they made it all the way through.

A few seconds after the doorway stopped grinding, it started closing again. It stayed open long enough for someone to get through and then automatically closed again.

The ceiling was higher in this new room, but Caleb still had to stoop slightly. The light in the room emanated from flashing monitors, the same type the Southern Marshal used to see what the Totos saw. The views on these screens were of the same low angled shots of various places in OZ. Whoever used this room was able to keep an eye on the world outside, just like the Southern Marshal did. He looked around the room and saw plenty of tables and shelves surrounding the wall of monitors, but no chairs.

"Dorothy?"

The voice came from the other side of the room and Caleb crouched in a defensive position, ready for anything.

Ready for anything, except what happened next.

A man in a wheelchair rolled out from behind the monitoring station. That would explain the lack of chairs.

The man's eyes lit up. "It is you!"

Dorothy and Caleb exchanged a look. She shook her head. He looked back at the man in the wheelchair.

"Her memory has been wiped, she doesn't remember you."

The man wheeled forward quickly, forcing them to take a step back before he ran over their toes. "Dorothy. It's me. William. William Sipes."

She struggled as she tried to access memories that were either deeply buried or gone. "I'm sorry. I don't remember anything."

He looked up at her, pleading. "You have to remember me!"

Caleb stepped in front of her. "The Southern Marshal gave her the scarecrow treatment. Everything's been erased. But we don't have time for that right now. We have to find someone called the Oracle."

The man in the wheelchair smiled. "You're looking at him."

"You're the Oracle?"

"Don't be so surprised."

"But Tara said the Oracle came from outside OZ. You're in a…"

William gripped the armrests of his chair. "I wasn't in this when I came into OZ. I came in on the same airship as Dorothy, but when the pirates attacked I fell out and woke up paralyzed from the waist down. Apparently I landed in a bale of hay, which save my life, but left me like this."

"She also said you knew the secret of OZ."

William squinted his eyes. "Is that what the Southern Marshal sent you to get?"

"I'm not sure."

William motioned to the numerous monitors along the wall. "These things are great at showing me what all the Totos see. But it's only visual. I don't have sound. I've gotten good at reading lips and I know the Southern Marshal sent the two of you on a quest. Is it for the weapon?"

"How do you know she sent us on a quest?"

"She let you out of the Southern Territories. From what I hear, she never does that. Ever. Are you after the weapon?"

"What do you know about the weapon?"

William laughed heartily. "My boy, it's why OZ exists."

That was an unexpected answer. "I thought OZ was a prison."

William rolled back and forth a couple of inches. "OZ is a prison. But that's its cover."

"It's cover?"

"When the people Dorothy's father and I worked for discovered that history's most powerful weapon had been hidden somewhere on the island continent to the south, they decided the best way to keep it safe was to make this a place nobody would willingly go and, if they ever ended up here, would never get out. Dorothy's father designed OZ so that nobody would come looking for the weapon here. The group we worked for, the Directors, destroyed all the records that pointed to the southern continent as the final resting place of this ancient weapon."

"Did you say the Directors?"

"Yes. You've heard of them?"

"According to the Southern Marshal, they are on their way right now to collect the weapon."

William frowned. "Why would they do that? They initiated the construction of OZ to keep it safe from the world."

"More like keep it for themselves. The man who raised me said he was sent by the Directors to locate the weapon. When he found out what it could do, he stalled them for as long as he could."

"What makes you think the Directors are coming for it?"

"Because Nero said they were. And they're going to be here in a matter of days. If I don't get to it first, they will have it. No one person should be able to wield that kind of power."

"Then why are you looking for it?"

"We have a plan to destroy it. Take it off the board completely."

William rolled back and forth, deep in thought. "Do you know where the weapon is now?"

"The Southern Marshal was hoping to find out before we made it to the Northern Territories. She thinks it's somewhere there."

"Why there?"

"Jasper took it and hid it."

"Who? I don't know a Jasper." William rolled over to the control panel in front of the monitors. He started flipping switches and turning dials. "But I might have an idea of who he is. I can't send a signal to control the Totos, but I'm able to intercept the transmission back. I can see everything the Southern Marshal is interested in looking at. She has had several Totos following this one boy, but I didn't know why."

A picture of a boy eating bread in some alley appeared on the main screen. William looked at him expectantly. "Is that Jasper?"

There was no mistaking the boy who was, at that moment, stuffing chunks of bread into his mouth. "Yeah, that's him."

The radio squelched on the wall behind them. William wheeled over to it quickly and flipped a switch. "Is everything set?"

Even through the static, it still sounded like Tara. "Everything's in place. I will be at the tube in one hour."

William flipped the switch and the static went silent. "We're going to help you get to that weapon before the Directors do. But first, we need to get your Tin Man back from the Banshees."

"And how do you propose we do that?"

William swung open the door of a wardrobe. An armored suit, similar to the one given to him by the Southern Marshal, and subsequently taken away by the Banshees, hung in the center of the wardrobe.

William smiled. "Not we. You."

Chapter 5

Caleb hefted the new suit out of the wardrobe. It was a lot heavier than the last suit.

William rolled back and forth in his wheelchair, clearly excited.

"I originally built the suit for me. For my escape. You'll notice the hydraulic assists on the joints. With my back broken, and my legs all but useless, I needed a way to walk again. Since you have the full use of your legs, the hydraulic assists will give you increased strength.

"I made a few modifications to Ben's original design. The jet packs on the back will enable you to fly for extended periods of time. No more just hopping around like a giant flea. It shouldn't take you too long to get used to it. Should you crash to the ground, don't worry. The suit will harden and you won't get anything more than a few bumps and bruises."

Caleb strapped on the pieces of armor while William helped him clamp the hydraulics in place. William focused on making sure every connection was sealed as he spoke quietly to Caleb.

"I think you should leave Dorothy here with me."

He couldn't do that. The Southern Marshal was adamant that Dorothy was needed to open the box that held the weapon.

"She's important. She has to come with me."

"I know what's at stake here, do you?"

What a strange question. He never would have agreed to this if he hadn't. "Of course I do."

William glanced over at Dorothy, seated in a dark corner, leaning against the wall with her eyes closed. "If she goes along…"

"She has to. She's the key to all this."

"That's exactly what I'm saying. If you take her with you, you will have to make a choice."

"A choice? Between what?"

"If I know her father, and I know him better than anyone, he locked the weapon inside a box that only she can open. As long as she lives, the world is in danger."

He did not like where this was going. "You are not killing her."

"I won't be the one killing her. If you get them both together in the same place, you, and you alone, will have to decide which to sacrifice. The world? Or her?"

He looked down at the man in the wheelchair. "She doesn't have to die."

William looked back up at him, sadness written over his entire face. "You can't save both."

A final click, followed by a hiss of air, signified the suit was ready.

One of the biggest changes over the previous suit was the complete protection offered. From the gloves, to the boots, and every joint, the suit covered him completely with the same hardening material that the previous armored plates were made from. This time, none of him would be exposed. Even better, the helmet, with its mirrored faceplate, hid his face as well as protected his head.

Caleb grabbed the helmet. "Yes I can."

He snapped on the helmet, locking it in place with a twist.

Tara flinched as the medic rubbed alcohol into the wound on her arm.

The High Priestess stood with her hands on her hips, her back to the roaring fireplace in the single-roomed house of the Oracle.

The High Priestess was eying her with suspicion. "You're telling me that Melissa attacked you?"

"Yes ma'am."

"That's interesting. She told me that you attacked her."

Tara did her best to look like she was controlling the rage building inside of her. "Who do you believe, ma'am?"

"I'm not sure which one of you to believe."

Time to put her service record to the ultimate test. "Have I ever given you reason to doubt my loyalties?"

The High Priestess pondered her question silently.

Time to spread it a little thicker. "Who, single-handedly, uncovered and foiled a plot to overthrow you five years ago?"

"We never caught the one who planned everything."

Time to drive the next nail in the coffin. "Who has turned down every opportunity for promotion?"

The High Priestess looked at Melissa, who leaned against the wall, still dazed from the electric shock. Even though she looked at Melissa, she addressed Tara. "Why do you think that is?"

"She claims it's so she can stay close to home to care for her ailing mother."

"She's not the only one who has refused promotion because of the increased responsibilities and commitment to the organization."

And... in for the kill. "It also means, there are no official reports on her activities outside the Banshees. Reports that you yourself requested after the failed attempt to end your regime. Refusing promotions kept her low enough in the organization to stay out of your reports. Her activities outside the organization might as well be a secret. A secret you should know."

From the look in the High Priestess eye, she knew she'd finally touched a nerve. There was one last thing to add to distract everyone long enough for the Southern Marshal's team to escape.

"And while you're asking her about that, find out what she did with the Oracle."

The High Priestess stormed over to Melissa and backhanded her across the face. "No more lies!"

Tara did her best to not let the smile inside register on her face. This was going better than planned. Everyone was so intent on watching the High Priestess interrogate one of their own, nobody noticed Tara slip out the front door.

In a massive natural underground cavern, torches burned brightly at intervals lighting up the entire space. Only deep crevices in the ceiling were still cast deep in shadow.

Caleb extricated himself from the debris of fallen rock. Moments before, he had slammed headfirst into a stalactite on the ceiling and plummeted to the floor of the cavern, rocks and chunks of earth raining down after him.

William was yelling from across the cavern. "Delicate movements! You keep over-correcting."

"Yeah, yeah," he muttered to himself as he ended up smearing the damp dirt across the front of the suit, instead of brushing it off.

William was relentless. "I built it to respond to me, and I'm paralyzed from the waist down. You're going to have to ease up on the controls. Try again."

Caleb flexed his neck back and forth. The suit did an excellent job of protecting him from the abuse he was putting it through now. He resisted the urge to close his eyes as he tried to envision flying in his mind again.

William tried to explain to him that the suit used biometric input rather than the mechanical input of his previous suit. He didn't need to crouch to activate this one. He just had to think about activating the flight jets, and magically it happened. William tried his best, and used big words in his attempt to prove it was not magic, about how electrical impulses from his brain were picked up by the helmet and amplified by any movement of his arms and legs.

No matter what William said, it still sounded like magic.

He thought about the jet pack integrated into the suit and rose a couple of feet in the air, hovering in place. He wobbled a lot less this time. Maybe he'd finally gotten the hang of it.

He eased himself forward and made a controlled ascent toward the ceiling. He tried very hard to concentrate on making delicate movements.

On the other side of the cavern, Dorothy held onto the handles on the back of William's wheelchair. Together, they watched Caleb swooping back and forth through the air.

She couldn't keep the excitement out of her voice. "I think he's got it."

Right then, he clipped a stalactite with his foot and spun out of control, straight for the ground. He hit the ground with such force, the impact cracked the rocky floor.

William shook his head. "Close enough."

Chapter 6

Caleb, Dorothy, and William stood on a low hill that overlooked Center City.

After several minutes of watching the distant city do nothing, Dorothy said exactly what Caleb was thinking. "What are we waiting for?"

William didn't take his eyes off the city. "Tara's signal."

Caleb peered through the tinted glass of his helmet. "What kind of signal are we waiting…"

He never finished his sentence as an explosion erupted on the outer edge of the city.

William pointed at the flames and black smoke that rolled skyward, as if everyone else had missed it. "There's the signal, and the diversion. Your robot is inside a warehouse on the opposite end of the city. You should meet with minimum resistance since everyone will be dealing with the fire."

Caleb took a deep breath when William placed a hand on his forearm. "Dorothy will be waiting for you at the tube. It will take you all the way to some friends in the Northern Territories."

"Are they going to help me?"

"I've explained to them what's at stake. They might still need a little convincing, but I think they will help."

William didn't sound too sure. "They will help? Or you think they will help?"

William poked him in the chest. "Just remember, you have the suit. It will protect you from any blunt force or piercing weapon. And it's been grounded to protect you from an electrical discharge weapon, like the gauntlets of the Banshees. I'm afraid it has no offense capabilities. I designed it primarily for escape, not really for combat."

Dorothy perked up at hearing this. "He could always just ram himself into the enemy."

William cracked a smile. "That's not a bad idea."

He slapped Caleb on the back, the suit absorbing the impact. "Now go, Tara's distraction won't keep them occupied forever."

Thank goodness for the mirrored faceplate on his helmet. It meant they could not see the worried look on his face. He took several steps away, he didn't want to burn them with the jet thrust, and imagined rocketing off valiantly into the sky.

He wanted to look the part of the hero as he flew to the rescue of the Tin Man. But the picture was ruined as his arms flailed about wildly while he spiraled up into the sky and arced toward the city.

The lack of a ceiling in the clear, open sky was the only thing keeping him from crashing into something. He focused on smooth, delicate movements and drew his arms in tightly.

He stopped corkscrewing through the air and actually managed to look like he knew what he was doing as he flew over the city wall.

The billowing smoke was to his right, so he angled slightly to the left, heading for the other side of the city where the Tin Man was waiting to be rescued.

Below him, Tara ran through the city opposite the throngs of people who ran against her, like a storm swelled river, to get a better view of the most exciting thing to happen in several months. Still dressed in her Banshee uniform, those that saw her quickly gave her right-of-way. Unfortunately, most of the people were fixated on the column of black smoke rising from the edge of the city and bumped into her without so much as an apology. She contemplated shocking a path ahead of her through the crowd with her gauntlet, but decided against drawing that much attention to the fact that she was running away.

The explosion had been much bigger than anticipated and the resulting fire was spreading quickly. She had very little time before she would have to explain what she was doing running away instead of helping to put the fires out.

She breathed a sigh relief as she reached the warehouse where the automaton was being kept. It was a large square building set apart from the rest of the buildings around it. She fished the key she had stolen out of a pocket and had just inserted it in the lock on the door when a roaring sound came up quickly behind her. She instinctively ducked out of the way just before something crashed through the door and disappeared into the warehouse.

She peeked around the splintered door frame at someone in a suit of armor picking himself up off the floor. This must be the suit the Oracle spoke of. The man in the suit spotted her and immediately adopted a defensive stance.

She stepped fully through the shattered doorway and kept her hands down at her side. She couldn't see through the mirrored faceplate, but the Oracle had informed her who to expect. "It's me, Tara. Are you the lion man?"

His voice echoed out through the breathing slots in his helmet as he inspected her more carefully and visibly relaxed. "Yes."

She nodded and pointed in the same direction she started walking. "Your robot is this way."

She crossed into the next room and froze, Caleb bumping into her from behind. He angled to the side to see why she had stopped so suddenly.

Standing between them and the Tin Man, was the High Priestess with ten Banshees on her right, and another ten on her left.

Chapter 7

Caleb and Tara faced down twenty Banshees in the middle of the warehouse. Just beyond them he could see the Tin Man locked up in a massive iron cage. Why was he standing in the dead center of his cage?

The bars looked thin enough that the Tin Man would have no problem prying them apart. The cages should have been able to contain its prisoner. But he wasn't trying to escape.

A small arc of electricity leaped from one bar to the next on the Tin Man's cage with a snapping sound. Well, that explained it. The bars, although thin and widely spaced, were electrified. The safest place was definitely the dead center of the cage.

But why hadn't the Tin Man destroyed the cage with his explosive bullets? It was then that Caleb noticed the ragged shards of metal where the gun had been forcibly torn from the Tin Man's arm. He was defenseless, and helpless inside that cage.

A sudden shove from behind alerted him to even more Banshees behind him. He quickly regained his balance, or was it the internal gyroscopes of the suit that kept him vertical? Whether he was improving, or it was the suit improving upon him, he was a better fighter, a better warrior, now than when he first woke up this morning in the hybrid colony.

He was tired of others pushing him around. It was time to take action. Time to be the leader everyone wanted him to be.

He squared his shoulders up and jutted his chin out defiantly, even though she couldn't see it inside his helmet.

"I am on an important quest and you need to let…"

She held up a hand, the electrified gauntlet hand, and he stopped talking. "I will speak with you in a moment."

Hands grabbed the arms of his suit from behind as others grabbed Tara and held them both in place while the High Priestess moved in closer to Tara.

"I had not expected it to be you. But then you went to great lengths to make me think it couldn't be you. You actually had me convinced you were on my side one hundred percent. And that makes what I'm about to do very difficult."

Tara opened her mouth to say something when lightning shot from the High Priestess' gauntlet and enveloped her in a crackling embrace. There had been no warning, and the two Banshees who had held on to Tara to prevent her escape were also caught up in the swirling electrical storm. The three women screamed and buckled to their knees, but the High Priestess did not let up.

Tendrils of smoke curled up from the edges of Tara's hair. Her clothes ignited in a burst of flame and she let out one final scream before collapsing in a charred heap on the floor, pulling the charred remains of the other two on top of her.

The High Priestess continued until Tara, and the two Banshees that were unfortunate enough to have held onto her, where nothing more than a pile of ash on the warehouse floor.

When she was satisfied her message had been received by everyone else in the room, she closed her hand and the crackle of electricity stopped.

Caleb stared at what remained of his only ally in Center City. A light breeze swept through the warehouse, lifted the white ash, and mixed it with the other piles of ash before spreading it thinly across the floor.

The High Priestess took a couple of steps closer to Caleb. The Banshees that held him quickly released their grip and scuttled out of the way, not wanting to become like the other two who had held on to Tara.

She peered at her own reflection in the mirrored visor of his helmet.

"Tell me about this weapon you are looking for."

Not her too. OZ was a big place until there was a juicy rumor about the ultimate weapon hidden within the prison's walls. And everybody who was hungry for ultimate power, of which OZ had a higher concentration of psychotic megalomaniacs than any other place on earth, was coming out of the woodwork. And they all wanted it.

The only one who didn't want it, was him.

She knocked on his visor. "Hello? Anybody home?"

He certainly wouldn't let her, or anyone who wanted to use it, get their hands on it.

She looked around at the other Banshees, a wry smile on her lips. "You think he fell asleep in there?"

She was expecting some form of answer from him. But if he wanted to get to that weapon and destroy it, before anyone else like her could obtain it, he had to give her an answer she never expected.

An answer that didn't require words.

He was outnumbered, and outgunned. His new suit had no offensive capabilities whatsoever, save for one.

The High Priestess raised her gauntlet. "I'm only going to ask you one more time."

Caleb leaned forward and envisioned the wide open spaces of the deep blue sky. His suit responded with full thrust.

At this angle, he shot forward, knocking over the High Priestess, and the rest of the Banshees in his way, like bowling pins.

William had mentioned the suit was grounded and could withstand a direct bolt of energy from a Banshee gauntlet. Caleb didn't know much about electricity, but maybe he could use his suit to short out the electrified bars on the Tin Man's cage. If he could get the Tin Man out of the cage, he could even out the odds a little better in his favor.

He slammed into the bars of the cage and felt a tingling sensation as his suit absorbed the energy being fed into the bars. It was not as heavily insulated as William had thought.

But then again, he was feeding it more energy than it was designed to withstand.

His hands gripped the bars and the suit trembled with the influx of energy. How much more could it take? He tried to pry his hands loose, but his fingers refused to cooperate and held on with an iron grip.

A scream from behind, sounding like someone shouting "Pirates!", was followed up by a deafening explosion that ripped his hands from the bars of the cage and sent him tumbling upward into the sky.

As he spun back down to earth, his eyes sought out the warehouse. Or more accurately, the burning crater where the warehouse used to be.

And resting just to the side of the fiery remains of the warehouse, the shadow of an airship. A trail of smoke started from a point in the empty sky and angled down in a straight line to what was left of the warehouse. The airship, hidden behind its sky colored camouflage, had given away its position when it launched its fiery missile.

All the delays he and his team had suffered gave the Directors' advance team time to catch up.

And he was still only halfway through OZ, with hundreds of kilometers between him and the ancient hybrid weapon. If this kept up, he would never get there before them.

He hit the ground. Landing hard on his back. The suit absorbed most of the impact, but his brain concussed heavily in his skull.

The last thing he saw before he lost consciousness was a portion of the sky rolling up like window blinds to reveal the airship hull dropping toward the ground, heading right for him.

The Adventure Continues...

Other Books by the Author

A is for Apprentice (Fantasy)

Oliver Twist: Victorian Vampire (Fantasy)

A Tale of Two Cities with Dragons (Fantasy)

Shade Infinity (Science Fiction Thriller)

Peacekeepers X-Alpha Series (Thriller)
    Inherit the Throne
    The Warrior's Code

Steampunk OZ Series (Science Fiction Serial)
        Forgotten Girl
        The Legacy's World
        Emerald Shadow
        The Future's Destiny

The Dangerous Captive

Missing Legacy

Shadow of History

The Edge of the Hunter

Fugue: The Cure (Science Fiction Short Story)

Stay informed about all the trouble I keep getting into. Subscribe to Steve DeWinter's Book Report (i.e. the mailing list) @ SteveDW.com